JEROME and the Witchcraft Kids

Welcome to the world, Olivia

Clarion Books
a Houghton Mifflin Company imprint
215 Park Avenue South, New York, NY 10003
Text and Illustrations copyright © 1988 by Eileen Christelow
All rights reserved.
For information about permission to reproduce
selections from this book, write to Permissions,
Houghton Mifflin Company, 2 Park Street, Boston, MA 02108
Printed in the USA

Library of Congress Cataloging-in-Publication Data
Christelow, Eileen.
Jerome and the Witchcraft kids.
Summary: Jerome Alligator's skill is put to the test
on Halloween night when he babysits Mrs. Witchcraft's
two devilish kids, Lucy and Lucifer.
[1. Halloween—Fiction.   2. Baby sitters—Fiction.
3. Alligators—Fiction].   I. Title.
PZ7.C4523Jc   1988   [E]   88-2597
ISBN 0-89919-742-6   PA ISBN 0-395-54428-9

WOZ   10 9 8 7 6 5 4 3 2

JEROME and the Witchcraft Kids

Eileen Christelow

Clarion Books
TICKNOR & FIELDS: A HOUGHTON MIFFLIN COMPANY
New York

On Halloween, Jerome was making posters.
On each one he wrote, "Jerome, the babysitter.
No job too difficult." And he pasted a picture of
himself in the center.

"Aren't you coming trick or treating?" asked
his sister Winifred. She was trying on costumes
with her best friend, Lulu.

"No, I'm too busy," said Jerome.

"Take a break," said Lulu. "Have a little fun."

"You already have more babysitting jobs than I do," grumbled Winifred. "I've been in business for three years and you've only been babysitting for three weeks."

"I'm a terrific babysitter," said Jerome. "Kids love me."

"Don't let it go to your head," said Lulu.
"Some day you might get a job that IS too difficult."

"I doubt it," said Jerome.

"What an interesting idea," Winifred said to herself.

While Jerome was out putting up his posters, Winifred and Lulu tried on some different costumes.

When Jerome came back, Winifred and Lulu were gone. He found a note on the door which said:

> Dear Jerome,
>   Can you babysit tonight from 6 to 8? If you can, come to the old yellow house at the edge of the swamp.
>   Desperately,
>   Mrs. Witchcraft

"How strange. I thought that house was empty," said Jerome. "Someone must have moved in."

At six Jerome rode his bike over to the old yellow house at the edge of the swamp. It was dark and quiet.

"I don't think anyone lives here," he said to himself. "It looks really spooky."

But he decided to knock on the door anyway.

The door opened.

"You're right on time," said a woman wearing a long, black dress and a tall, black hat.

"Maybe I have the wrong house," gasped Jerome.

"No, I'm Mrs. Witchcraft," cackled the woman. "This is the right house. Come in and meet the children."

The house was so dark, it was difficult to see the children.

"This is Lucy and this is Lucifer," said Mrs. Witchcraft. "Supper is in the refrigerator and be sure they take a bath."

"Don't worry," said Jerome. "I will."

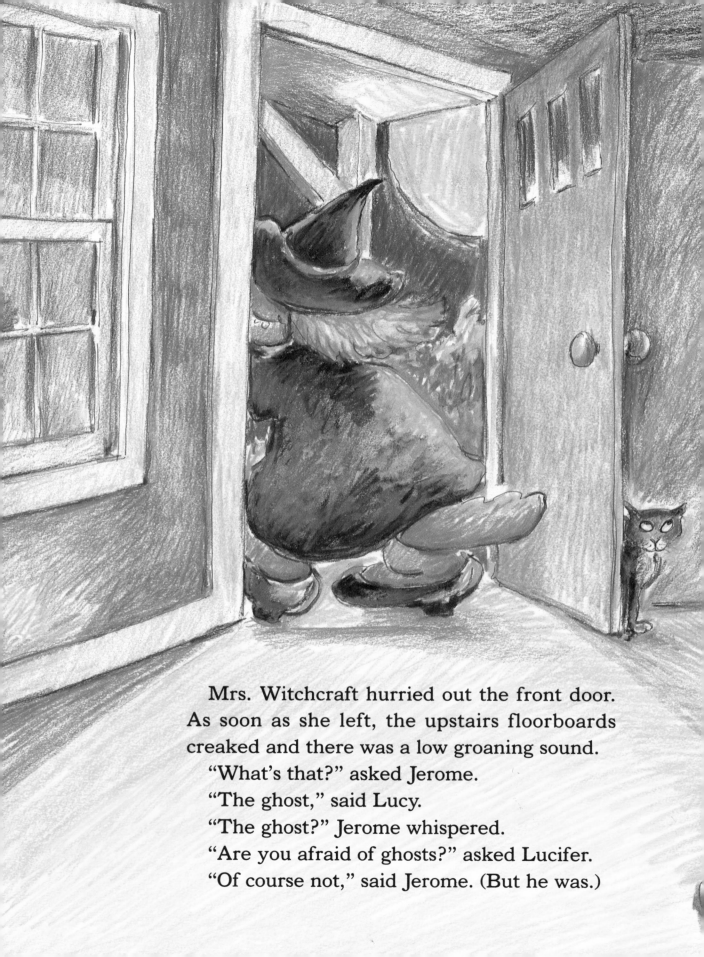

Mrs. Witchcraft hurried out the front door. As soon as she left, the upstairs floorboards creaked and there was a low groaning sound.

"What's that?" asked Jerome.

"The ghost," said Lucy.

"The ghost?" Jerome whispered.

"Are you afraid of ghosts?" asked Lucifer.

"Of course not," said Jerome. (But he was.)

Jerome was shaking so much, he could barely open the refrigerator to look for supper. And he almost fainted when he saw the jar of lizard's eyeballs, the bowl of dead worms, and the bottle of vampire blood.

"Yum!" said Lucy and Lucifer. "We want eyeball sandwiches."

"Don't you have any peanut butter?" groaned Jerome.

Jerome held his breath and tried to close his eyes when he made the sandwiches. Lucy and Lucifer helped.

"I like vampire blood on my eyeballs," said Lucy. "Me too," giggled Lucifer.

Lucy and Lucifer were messy eaters. Eyeballs popped out of their sandwiches and rolled on the floor. Vampire blood and worms oozed all over their clothes, hands, and faces.

"Now you have to give us a bath," said Lucy.

"The bathtub is upstairs," said Lucifer. "Where the ghost stays."

"I'm not afraid of ghosts," said Jerome. (But he was.)

He crept upstairs. Lucy and Lucifer followed. The floorboards creaked. Jerome stopped.

"Go on!" said Lucy and Lucifer. They pushed him up the stairs to the bathroom door.

But someone was already in the tub. "It's the ghost!" shrieked Jerome.

"It's going to get us," cried Lucifer. They all raced down the stairs.

"Hide in the basement!" shouted Lucy. She held open the basement door.

Jerome ran down the steps. A bat brushed against his nose. He jumped away, tripped over something on the floor, and fell into the sheets that were hanging on the laundry line.

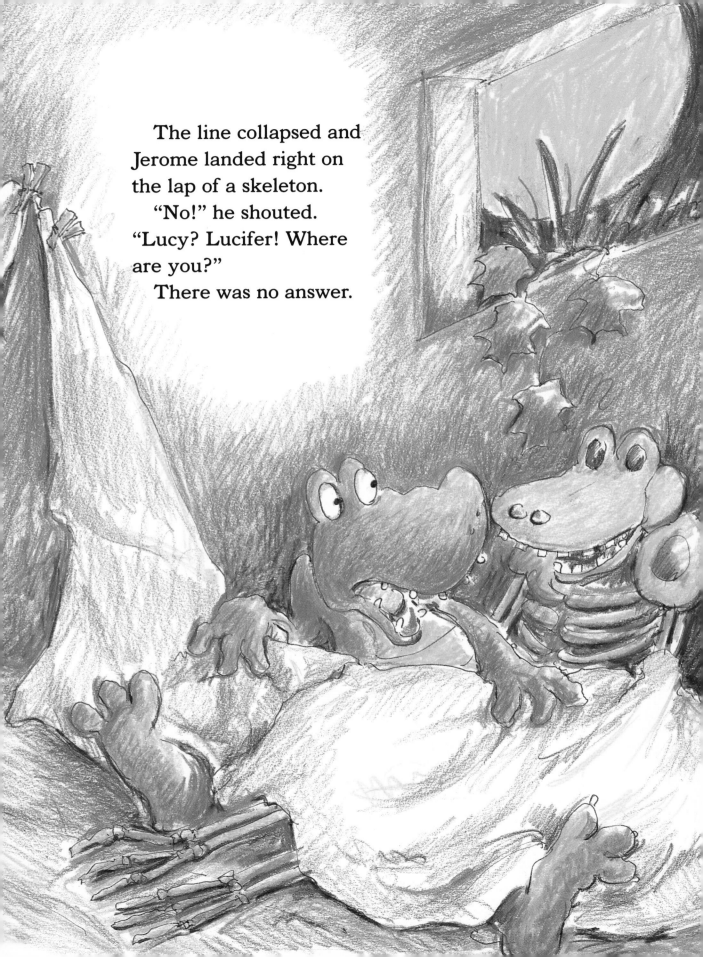

The line collapsed and
Jerome landed right on
the lap of a skeleton.
"No!" he shouted.
"Lucy? Lucifer! Where
are you?"
There was no answer.

Jerome scrambled back up the steps. The basement door was locked. He heard voices, so he peeked through a crack in the door.

"It's Winifred and Lulu!" gasped Jerome. "And Lulu's little sisters. I've been tricked!"

He listened carefully. "He really thought I was Mrs. Witchcraft," Lulu was saying.

"And he thought the peeled grapes were eyeballs and he nearly fainted when he saw Winifred in the bathtub, dressed as a ghost," said Lulu's little sisters.

"And did you hear me creaking the floor-boards?" said Winifred.

"Shall we let him out of the basement now?" asked Lulu.

"In a few more minutes," giggled Winifred.

But then they heard the front door open behind them.

"A ghost!" whispered Winifred. They were all so scared they couldn't move.

The ghost raised its arms and floated toward them.

"Guess whooooo?" it screeched.

"Jerome?" gasped Winifred. "How did you get here?"

"I borrowed a sheet from the laundry line," said Jerome. "Then I climbed out the basement window and decided to scare *you* for a change."

"Well, you certainly did!" said Lulu.

Just then, the floorboards creaked upstairs
and they heard a low, moaning sound.

"What's that?" asked Jerome.

"It's not me this time," said Winifred.

"Let's get out of here!" said Lulu.

And they did!